KT-230-131

Mighty Machines
FIRE ENGINE

02 | 26

075 135 604 241 08

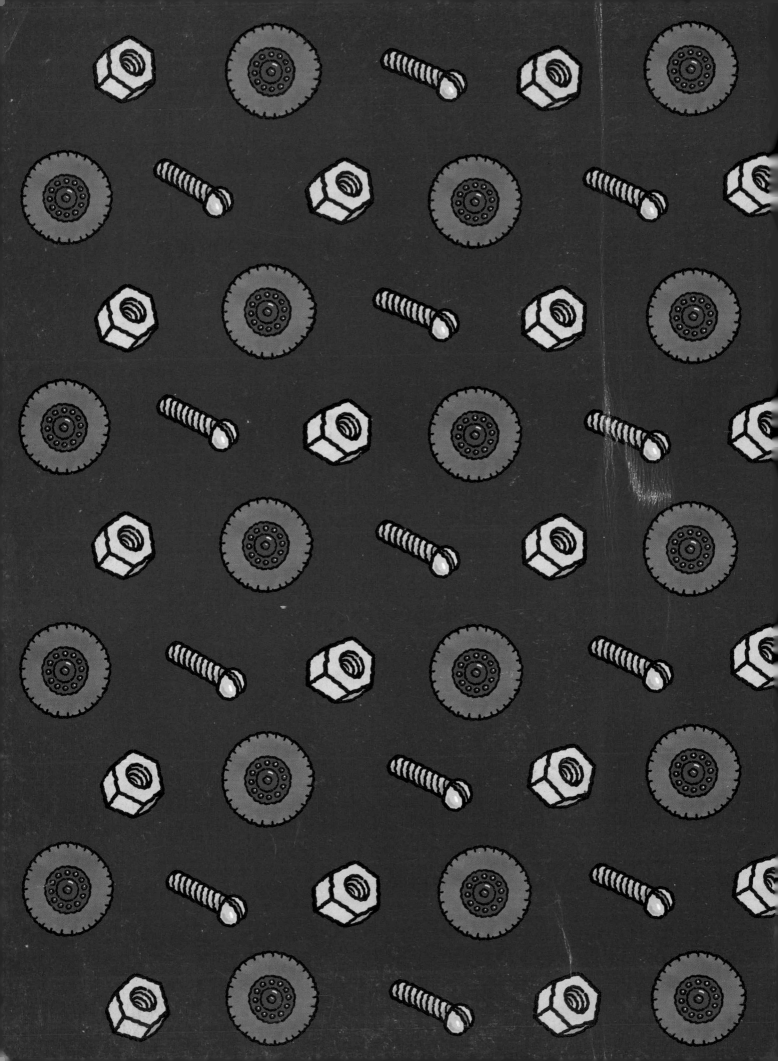

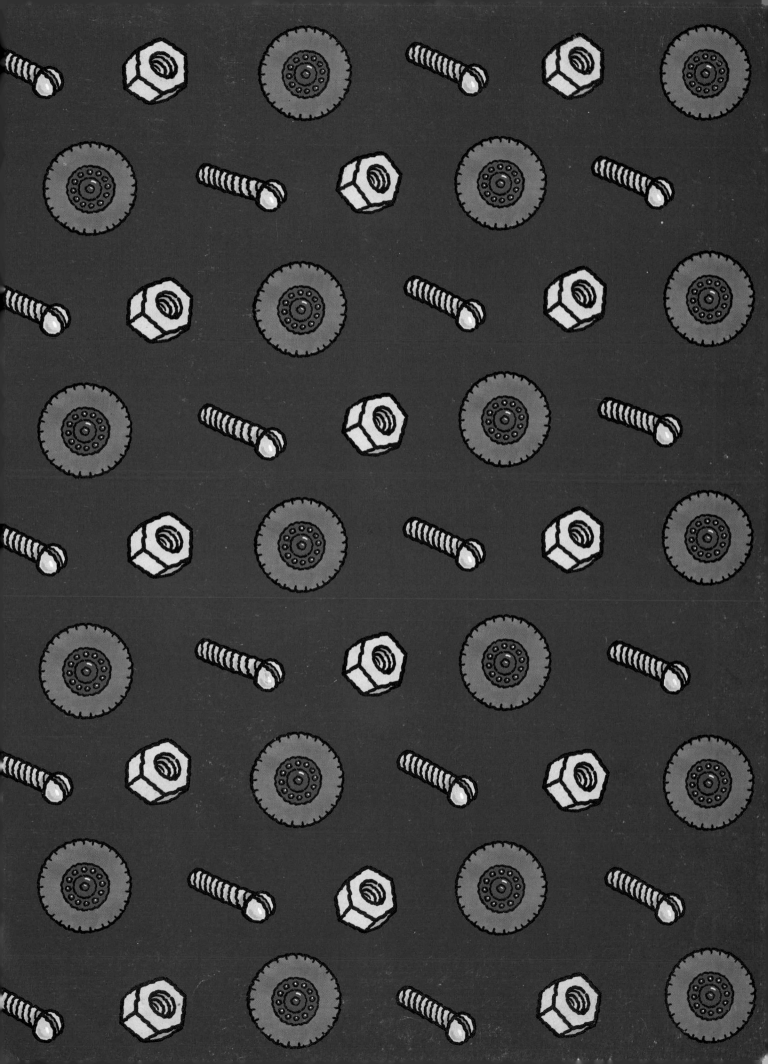

A DORLING KINDERSLEY BOOK

Editor Mary Ling
Designer Claire Penny
Managing Editor Sheila Hanly
Production Josie Alabaster
Photography Lynton Gardiner
Illustrator Ellis Nadler
Consultant Product Engineer
David Tennies, Seagrave Fire
Apparatus, Inc.

Published in Great Britain
by Dorling Kindersley Limited,
9 Henrietta Street, London WC2E 8PS

Paperback edition
4 6 8 10 9 7 5 3

Copyright © 1995, 1998 Dorling Kindersley Limited

Visit us on the World Wide Web at
http://www.dk.com

All rights reserved. No part of this publication
may be reproduced, stored in a retrieval system,
or transmitted in any form or by any means,
electronic, mechanical, photocopying,
recording or otherwise, without the prior
written permission of the copyright owner.

A CIP catalogue record for this book
is available from the British Library.

ISBN: 0-7513-5604-2

Colour reproduction by Chromagraphics, Singapore
Printed and bound in Italy by L.E.G.O.

The publisher would like to thank the following for
their kind permission to reproduce their
photographs:
t=top, b=bottom, c=centre, l=left, r=right

Canadair: 20b; Image Bank/Larry Dale Gordon: 4tl,
20tl; Robert Harding: 21c; Richard Leeney: 2br, 3br,
9t, 13t, 16/17c; Ray Moller: 3bl, 10/11c

Every effort has been made to trace the copyright
holders and we apologize in advance for any
unintentional omissions. We would be pleased to
insert the appropriate acknowledgement in any
subsequent edition of this publication.

Scale
Look out for drawings
like this – they show
the size of the machines
compared with people.

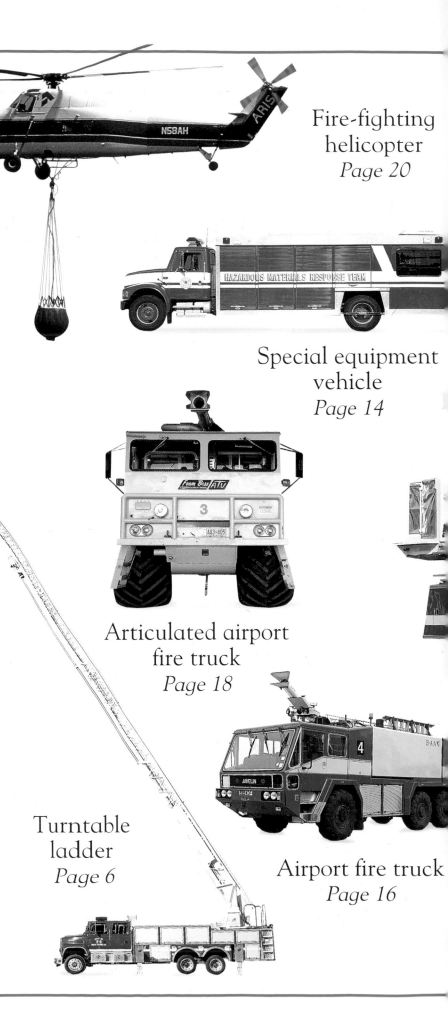

Fire-fighting
helicopter
Page 20

Special equipment
vehicle
Page 14

Articulated airport
fire truck
Page 18

Turntable
ladder
Page 6

Airport fire truck
Page 16

Mighty Machines

FIRE ENGINE

Caroline Bingham

Hydraulic platform
Page 8

Water tender
engine
Page 10

Rapid intervention
vehicle
Page 13

DK
DORLING KINDERSLEY
LONDON • NEW YORK • MOSCOW • SYDNEY

Fire engine

AMAZING FACTS

🔩 A fire engine's siren is as loud as a clap of thunder booming above!

🔩 Telescopic ladders can stretch out to 41 metres. That's as high as 34 seven-year-old children – if they could stand on top of each other!

Scale

A fire engine is built to rush firefighters and their equipment to the scene of a fire. Lights flash and a siren sounds as the engine speeds along.

cab

the ladder has wide safety rails

fire crew's compartment

105 FT

NEW ROCHELLE 13

NEW ROCHELLE FIRE DEPT Co 13

Pierce

NEW

Turntable ladder

This fire engine is called a turntable ladder. It carries a giant ladder which extends telescopically. Some fire engines have ladders that can reach up to the 11th floor of a high-rise building.

Scale

safety rails

big mirrors help the driver to see behind when reversing

the ladder sits on a giant turntable

A **turntable** is a raised platform that can swivel round to help position the ladder.   7

Hydraulic platform

AMAZING FACTS

Some snorkel booms can reach to 62 metres – that's as high as 20 balancing giraffes!

Fire engines known as hydraulic platforms, or snorkels, have a long arm called a boom. This is built in two or three sections so it unfolds to reach awkward places. It can go up and over to the back of a burning building, or reach down over the side of a bridge. At the end of the boom is a platform for rescuing people.

Scale

extension ladders

Extension ladders pull out to two or three times their stored length.

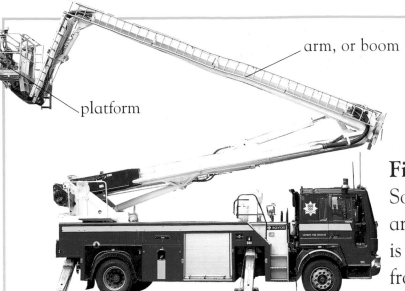

arm, or boom

platform

leg

Firm footing

Some fire engines have legs which are put down each time the boom is raised. They stop the engine from rocking about or falling over.

arm with built-in hose

Water from above

A flexible, built-in hose runs up the arm of a snorkel to a nozzle. Water travels through the hose and rains down on a fire from above.

siren

A **hose** is a hollow tube.   A **nozzle** directs the water jet at the fire.

Water tender engine

A water tender engine, or pumper, carries enough water and foam to put out a small fire, such as a car fire. It also has a pump to bring water from the main underground water supply. Firefighters attach hoses to street hydrants to reach this water.

Street hydrants are like giant taps to the main water supply.

extension ladders are carried on the roof of the pumper

equipment locker

hoses are kept neatly rolled up

long lengths of hose are carried on a pumper

A **pump** increases the pressure, or force, of water passing through the hoses.

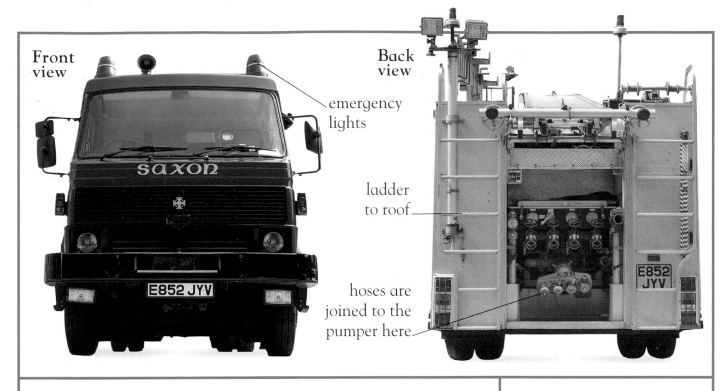

Front view

emergency lights

SAXON

E852 JYV

Back view

ladder to roof

hoses are joined to the pumper here

E852 JYV

rear-view mirror

a step helps the driver climb into the cab

fire crew's compartment

AMAZING FACTS

Before machine-powered pumps were invented, water was pumped by hand. Some large pumps needed 50 men to operate them.

A pumper carries 1,365 litres of water – you could enjoy a shower for five hours with that much water.

Foam is used to extinguish certain types of fire, such as burning oil and petrol.

Reaching a fire

Scale

Easy to spot!
All fire engines have emergency lights. When other road users see these lights flash, they know the engine is in a hurry and wants to pass.

Firefighters have to hurry when they get an emergency call. When there is a big fire, the fire chief rushes to the scene in a special fast car. The chief takes charge and decides exactly what equipment is needed to put out the fire.

warning lights

the car has a powerful engine under the bonnet

GMC

NEW YORK
A28790
OFFICIAL

headlights flash as the chief's car moves through traffic

An **engine** burns a fuel, such as petrol, to make a vehicle move.

Rapid intervention vehicle (RIV)

Fast response is vital at airport fires. The RIV races to an accident before the bigger trucks. It carries enough foam and water to spray for about five minutes.

floodlight

3

AMAZING FACTS

🔩 Firefighters can respond to a call and be out of their station in 20 seconds. It takes longer than that to tie your shoelaces.

🔩 An RIV can accelerate from 0–112 kilometres per hour in seven seconds – as fast as a sports car.

a fire vehicle's tyre pressure is frequently checked so the vehicle grips the road properly

🔩 The correct **tyre pressure** means the vehicle's tyres have the right amount of air. 🔩 13

Special equipment vehicles

AMAZING FACTS

🔩 Cutting equipment carried on a rescue vehicle can slice into a metal car as easily as a tin opener cuts into a tin can. It takes less than 60 seconds to cut off a car's roof.

🔩 Firefighters can "see" through thick smoke and heavy rubble with a special camera.

Special equipment is needed to fight a petrol, chemical, or electrical fire because water will not put out this type of fire. Hazardous materials trucks carry this equipment in big lockers.

Scale

emergency lights

giant patches to seal leaking containers

traffic cones

box for small tools

chemical foams

🔩 A **locker** is a safe place for storage. 🔩 **Traffic cones** are used to control traffic. 🔩

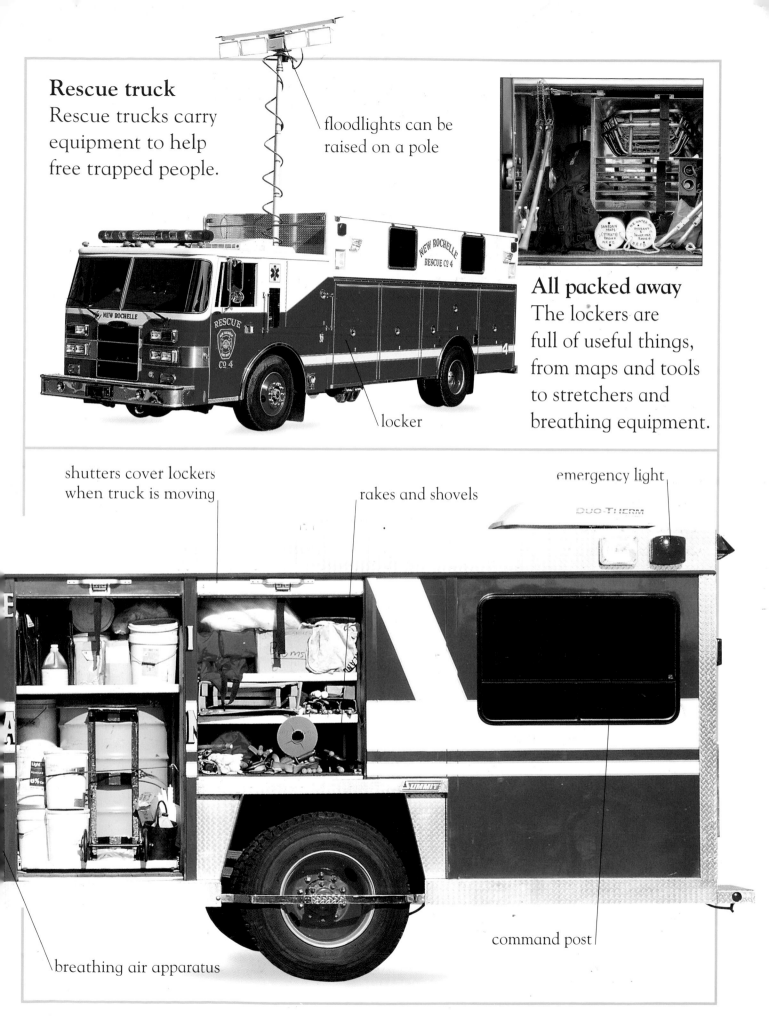

Rescue truck

Rescue trucks carry equipment to help free trapped people.

floodlights can be raised on a pole

All packed away
The lockers are full of useful things, from maps and tools to stretchers and breathing equipment.

locker

shutters cover lockers when truck is moving

rakes and shovels

emergency light

command post

breathing air apparatus

Floodlights light up large areas so people can work at night.

Airport fire truck

Airport fires are especially dangerous because a plane may have a full tank of highly flammable fuel. Airport fire trucks can answer a call and put out a fire within two minutes!

monitor

AMAZING FACTS

A central steering wheel gives the driver good all-round vision.

The telescopic floodlight is as bright as 30,000 candles!

An airport truck carries 10,000 litres of water. If you drink one litre of water a day, it will take more than 27 years to get through 10,000 litres!

JAVELIN

E189 KDF

GLOSTER SARO

sloped shape helps the truck to cross bumpy ground

Fuel is highly **flammable**, which means it burns very easily.

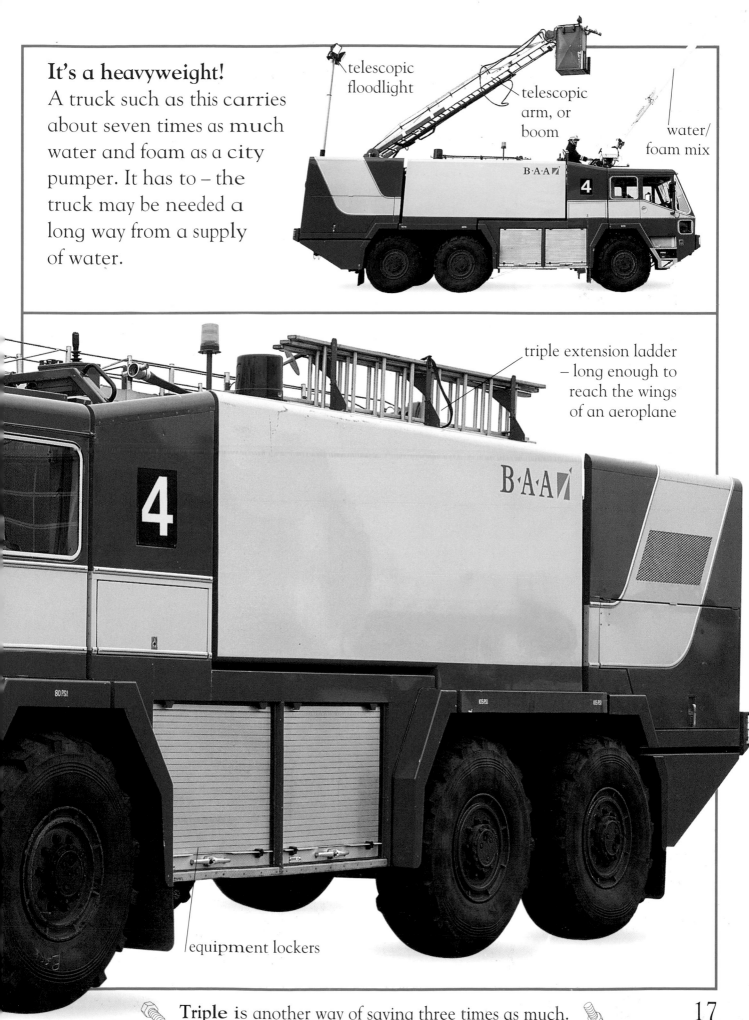

It's a heavyweight!

A truck such as this carries about seven times as much water and foam as a city pumper. It has to – the truck may be needed a long way from a supply of water.

telescopic floodlight

telescopic arm, or boom

water/foam mix

triple extension ladder – long enough to reach the wings of an aeroplane

equipment lockers

Triple is another way of saying three times as much.

Articulated airport fire truck

Monster-sized fire trucks guard big international airports. This giant, fast moving airport truck is articulated, which means it can bend in the middle. This helps it move safely over the bumpy ground between runways.

Scale

monitor with moveable arm

articulated for rough ground

Foam Boss A.T.V.
CDM RESEARCH-CANADA

3

0396

AA3-405
ONTARIO

Transport Canada Transports Canada

Canada

58-7901

A **monitor** acts like a nozzle, directing a water jet.

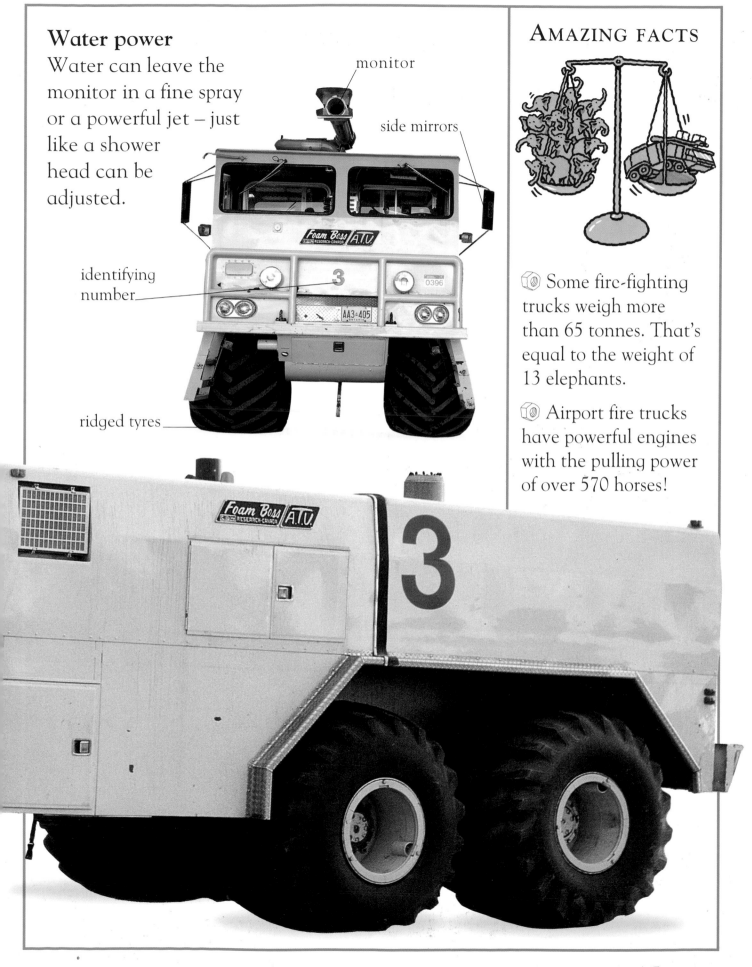

Water power

Water can leave the monitor in a fine spray or a powerful jet – just like a shower head can be adjusted.

monitor

side mirrors

identifying number

ridged tyres

Foam Boss A.T.V.

3

0396

AA3=405

Some fire-fighting trucks weigh more than 65 tonnes. That's equal to the weight of 13 elephants.

Airport fire trucks have powerful engines with the pulling power of over 570 horses!

Foam Boss A.T.V.

3

An **articulated** truck has two sections so it can bend over bumps in its path.

Air and sea firefighters

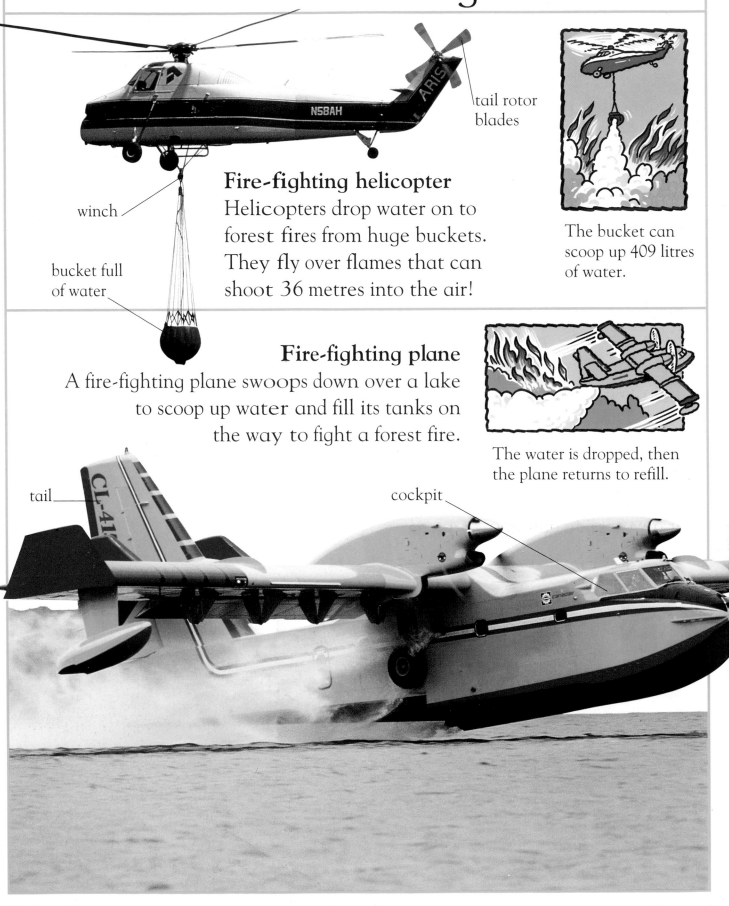

tail rotor blades

winch

bucket full of water

Fire-fighting helicopter
Helicopters drop water on to forest fires from huge buckets. They fly over flames that can shoot 36 metres into the air!

The bucket can scoop up 409 litres of water.

Fire-fighting plane
A fire-fighting plane swoops down over a lake to scoop up water and fill its tanks on the way to fight a forest fire.

The water is dropped, then the plane returns to refill.

tail

cockpit

A pilot sits in a **cockpit.** A **winch** is used to raise and lower objects.

powered
jet of water

Fireboat

Fireboats
patrol harbours
and rivers. They
can pump enormous
quantities of water
from the river to squirt
on to a burning boat
or a waterside building.

bridge

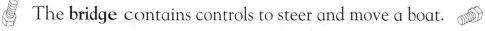

The **bridge** contains controls to steer and move a boat.

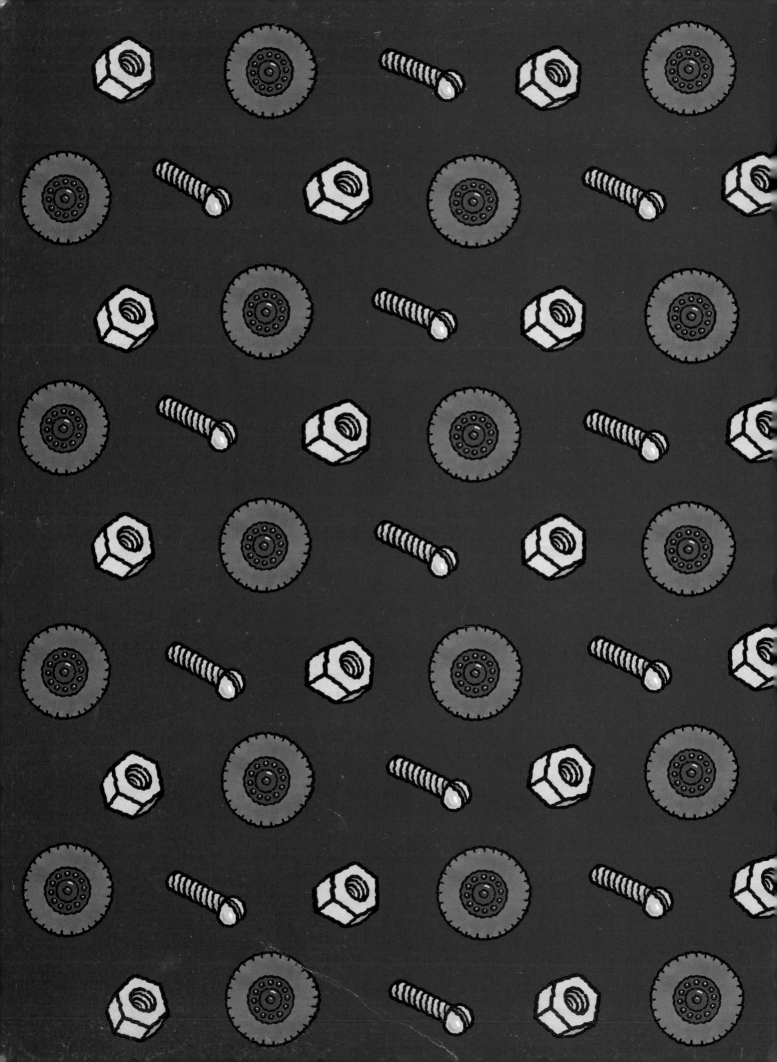

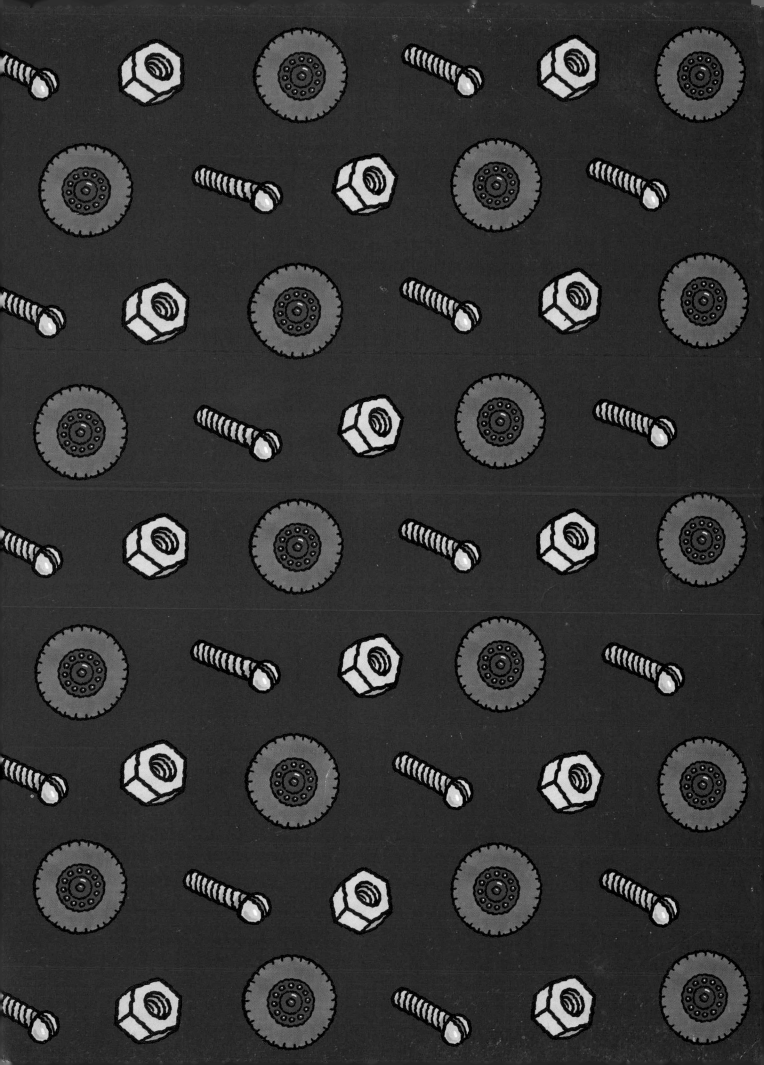